# Rainbow Monsters

Written by Sylva Fae
Illustrations by Sylva
and the little Fae

# Copyright

## Dedication

For my own little monsters:
Scarlett, Sienna and Sylva

## With thanks to:

Dave for your patience, support and
technical elf skills.

Authors Suzanne Downes, N.G.K.
Cusper Lynn and Susan Faw for your
friendship, support and inspiration.

And a big thank you to the wonderful
members of the IASD for always having
the answers and delivering them with
good humour.

On a mixed up rainy, sunny day,

The rainbow monsters love to play.

Sliding down their coloured light,

These monsters really are a sight.

Racing clouds down to the ground,
The monsters land and dance around.

While sun shines and rain falls down,
They fly through fields and into town.

Meet the monsters, Green and Blue,

Red and Yellow, Orange too.

With Violet and Indigo,

They make the monster fun rainbow.

Little Red's a sleepy head,
She likes to curl up in her bed.
She falls asleep unless she's fed,
On ice-cream, buns and jammy bread.

Orange bounces like a ball.

He's round and cute, no feet at all.

When he boings you hear him call,

"Watch out below, I'm going to fall!"

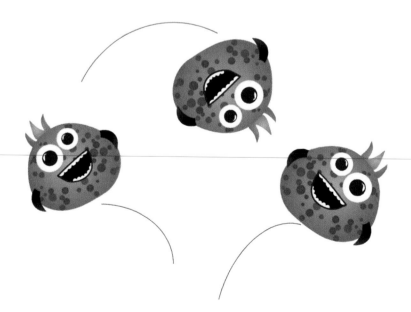

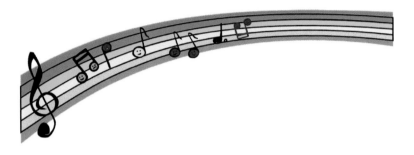

This monster is a happy fellow.
He likes his music nice and mellow,
Playing tunes upon his cello,
Sing along with smiley Yellow.

Take a look at pretty Green,

Her curly fur is shiny clean.

She loves to show off and be seen,

This monster is a beauty queen.

Blue's a rascal, funny too.

He's up to mischief, yes it's true.

He'll play a trick on me and you.

Beware of cheeky monster Blue!

This is sparkly Indigo,

Her glittered fur's a shiny glow.

Twinkly, purple shimmers flow,

The brightest of the whole rainbow.

Here's splishy, splashy Violet.

She's happy when she's getting wet.

A puddle jumping muddy pet,

The muckiest you'll ever get.

On a mixed up sunny, rainy day,

Rainbow monsters laugh and play.

These monsters really are a sight,

Leaving trails of coloured light.

You've met monsters, Green and Blue,

Red and Yellow, Orange too.

With Violet and Indigo,

They make the monster fun rainbow.

But now the sun has gone away,

The monsters really cannot stay.

The rainbow fades behind the cloud,

Wave goodbye to the monster crowd.

# Fun and Games with the Rainbow Monsters

## Unscramble these anagrams

| bianrow | stormen | voteli |
|---------|---------|--------|
| nereg | rogena | yollew |
| der | Lueb | dignio |

# Can you find a home
## for each of the
## Rainbow Monsters?

# How many red things can you find?

# Red

# How many orange things can you find?

Orange

# How many yellow things can you find?

Yellow

# How many green things can you find?

## Green

# How many blue things can you find?

# Blue

# How many indigo things can you find?

# Indigo

# How many violet things can you find?

# Violet

# Can you help Orange find his friend Blue?

# Monster Wordsearch

| R | E | D | H | S | S | K | Y |
|---|---|---|---|---|---|---|---|
| A | R | F | A | U | S | T | E |
| I | N | G | K | N | B | C | L |
| N | S | U | Z | E | L | L | L |
| B | S | E | I | R | U | O | O |
| O | R | A | N | G | E | U | W |
| W | A | O | D | J | R | D | U |
| L | I | N | I | C | O | L | S |
| I | N | P | G | R | E | E | N |
| G | V | I | O | L | E | T | I |
| H | F | A | W | F | U | N | A |
| T | M | O | N | S | T | E | R |

| | | |
|---|---|---|
| RED | INDIGO | MONSTER |
| ORANGE | VIOLET | FUN |
| YELLOW | RAINBOW | CLOUD |
| GREEN | SUN | RAIN |
| BLUE | SKY | LIGHT |

# About The Author

Sylva Fae is a married mum of three from Lancashire, England. She grew up in a rambling old farmhouse with a slightly dysfunctional family and an adopted bunch of equally dysfunctional animals.

As a qualified lecturer and verifier, she has spent twenty years teaching literacy to adults with learning difficulties and disabilities.

Sylva and her husband own a wood where they run survival courses and woodland craft days. Adventures in the woods inspired her to write stories to entertain her three girls.

Sylva Fae writes a blog about her woodland escapades with the little Fae:

## sylvafae.co.uk

If you've enjoyed this book,
And loved the monsters too,
Please make an author happy,
And leave a short review.

# Coming Soon...

Book two in the Rainbow Monsters series:

## Mindful Monsters

# Recommendations from
# my little Monsters

When my little monsters aren't helping to
write 'Mummy Stories', they love reading
the Harry The Happy Mouse series,
written by N.G.K. and illustrated by
Janelle Dimmett.

They're available in paperback, and free
to download as Kindle and audio books.

**harrythehappymouse.com**

Printed in Great Britain
by Amazon